TWO of a kind™ Diaries

Win a
cool sterling silver
charm bracelet!
Details on page 97.

Look for more

titles:

TWO of a kind™

Diaries

Candles, Cake, Celebrate!

by Judy Katschke
from the series created by
Robert Griffard & Howard Adler

HarperEntertainment
An Imprint of HarperCollinsPublishers
A PARACHUTE PRESS BOOK

A PARACHUTE PRESS BOOK

Parachute Publishing, L.L.C.
156 Fifth Avenue
Suite 302
New York, NY 10010

Published by
HarperEntertainment
An Imprint of HarperCollins*Publishers*
10 East 53rd Street, New York, NY 10022-5299

TWO OF A KIND books created and produced by
Parachute Press, L.L.C., in cooperation with Dualstar Publications,
a division of Dualstar Entertainment Group, LLC,
published by HarperEntertainment, an imprint of HarperCollins Publishers.

ISBN 0-06-059591-4

First printing: February 2005

Printed in the United States of America

Visit HarperEntertainment on the World Wide Web at
www.harpercollins.com

10 9 8 7 6 5 4 3 2 1

Chapter 1

Tuesday

Dear Diary,

I love surprises. Surprise parties, surprise phone calls from friends, sometimes even the meat loaf surprise in the school dining room. But surprises don't mean a thing to my sister. That's because no matter how hard I try, Mary-Kate just can't be surprised!

But this morning at breakfast, I decided to give it another shot.

"Hi, guys!" I said. I sat down at our usual table in the dining room. "How's the banana-nut oatmeal?"

"Let's just say you'll need a fork," Mary-Kate said as she poked at her bowl. "It's extra lumpy today!"

Oatmeal for breakfast is a big tradition here at the White Oak Academy for Girls in New Hampshire. It's hard to believe that our boarding school has been around for more than a hundred years. Maybe that's why our dining room looks like the inside of an old castle!

I glanced around the table at our friends. Cheryl Miller, Summer Sorensen, Phoebe Cahill, and Elise Van Hook all looked half-asleep as they swirled their spoons in their oatmeal.

"I'm still zonked out from that statewide history test we studied for all weekend," Cheryl said with a half-yawn.

"I'm just glad it's over." My roommate Phoebe groaned as she buttered her toast. "All those names to remember!"

Phoebe was wearing a denim miniskirt, purple cowboy boots, and tights with a black-and-white pattern that made me dizzy. Phoebe's way-cool clothes are all vintage. Sometimes I tease her that "vintage" is just a fancy word for hand-me-down!

"And all those dates! Like 1492, 1776, 1812!" Elise said. "I am so horrible at remembering dates!"

"Unless they're with Peter Juarez!" Mary-Kate teased.

Elise lowered her eyes and blushed. Peter is her boyfriend at the Harrington Academy for Boys, right down the road from our school.

All this talk about history tests and boys was distracting me from my plan. If I was going to start surprising Mary-Kate, I was going to have to start now. . . .

"Mary-Kate, forget about your lumpy banana-nut oatmeal," I declared. "Because this is your lucky day!"

"Why?" Mary-Kate asked. She glanced back at the kitchen. "Are there banana-nut muffins instead?"

I shook my head and said, "Something better. I have a surprise for you!"

"I love surprises!" Summer said. Her smile gleamed white against her California tan. "What is it, Ashley?"

"Summer!" Cheryl said. She rolled her dark eyes. "It wouldn't be a surprise if she said what it was."

"What do you think it is, Mary-Kate?" I asked. "Go ahead. Guess."

"Hmm," Mary-Kate said. She pressed her lips together and narrowed her eyes as she thought.

I held my breath.

Mary-Kate doesn't seem to have a clue! I thought. *Could this be it? Is she about to be surprised for the first time in our lives?*

"Let's see," Mary-Kate said slowly. Her blue eyes lit up, and she snapped her fingers. "Is it a peanut butter-chocolate energy bar with vanilla-yogurt icing?"

My jaw dropped. She did it again! Mary-Kate guessed another surprise!

"Well?" Mary-Kate asked with a smirk. "Is it?"

All eyes were on me as I pulled a peanut butter-chocolate energy bar with vanilla-yogurt icing from my bag. I tossed it on the table, saying, "You got it."

Our friends went totally wild.

"No way!" Elise squealed.

3

"How did you know that, Mary-Kate?" Phoebe asked.

Mary-Kate tore open the energy bar and took a bite. "Because I saw it in Ashley's bag yesterday," she said between chews.

"You saw it in my bag?" I asked, disappointed.

Summer clapped her hands and squealed, "Mary-Kate has X-ray vision, everybody. Just like Superman!"

"I don't have X-ray vision, Summer," Mary-Kate said. "Ashley was carrying her light blue jelly bag yesterday, and I could see right into it."

I gulped. Mary-Kate was right. My light blue jelly bag is practically transparent!

"Plus, Ashley hates yogurt icing on anything," Mary-Kate went on. "So I figured it must be for me."

I shook my head and said, "I should have known you can never be surprised. What was I thinking?"

"That's crazy, Ashley," Cheryl said. "Everybody can be surprised."

"Everybody but Mary-Kate," I said. "Back home in Chicago, Mary-Kate's softball team won a city-wide championship. So I invited all of our friends from school to a surprise party for Mary-Kate."

"I remember," Mary-Kate said with a grin.

"We all heard Mary-Kate coming into the house," I went on. "We turned off the lights in the living

4

room and hid behind the chairs and sofa. But Mary-Kate walked in the room, turned on the lights, and yelled, 'What a surprise!'"

"So she *was* surprised," Cheryl said.

"Not exactly," I said. "Mary-Kate yelled it out before we even jumped out!"

"How did you . . . ?" Phoebe started to say.

"It was a no-brainer," Mary-Kate explained. "I saw all the jackets hanging in the hall. And a stack of pizza boxes in the kitchen."

"You see?" I said to my friends.

"Hey, don't sweat it, Ashley," Mary-Kate said. "I guess I'm just naturally . . . unsurprisable!"

A crackling noise filled the dining room. That meant an announcement was about to come across the loudspeaker.

"Good morning, girls," a cheery voice said.

It was Mrs. Pritchard. She's the headmistress of the White Oak Academy. Sometimes we call her "the Head."

"Good morning, Mrs. Pritchard!" Summer replied.

"Summer!" Cheryl said with a laugh. "She can't hear you."

Most of the other students kept on eating. But some actually turned to face the loudspeaker.

"A few quick announcements," Mrs. Pritchard

said. "There will be a meeting of the Student Council after last period today. The Glee Club is selling raffle tickets during each lunch period all this week. Don't forget that your class evaluations will be due at the end of this month. And finally, I would like Mary-Kate Burke to please see me in my office after breakfast. Thank you, and enjoy your oatmeal."

Click.

Everyone stared at Mary-Kate—including me, Diary!

"Omigosh, Mary-Kate," Elise whispered. "What did you do?"

Mary-Kate sat frozen in her chair. She shook her head slowly. "I don't know!" she said. "Maybe I forgot to clean out my gym locker. Or maybe I've been taking too many mustard packets for my turkey sandwiches. Or maybe I'm playing my rock music too loud!"

"Or maybe it's something good!" I said with a hopeful smile.

"Ashley, no one is ever called into the Head's office for doing something good," Mary-Kate said. "Maybe I forgot to return a library book. Or a—"

"Blueberry muffin?" A soft voice cut in.

I glanced up and saw our friend Lavender Duncan. She was wearing a crisp white apron over her sweater and jeans. And she was holding a tray piled high with muffins.

"They're still warm, and I used extra-big blueberries, too," Lavender said, smiling.

Lavender has a lot to smile about these days. She has her own crafts, cooking, and party-planning column in the First Form newspaper, the White Oak *Acorn*. And if that wasn't enough, Lavender is about to launch her own Web site. She's always doing nice things for all of us, like baking these muffins.

"I baked them this morning, using a recipe I came up with in my cooking class yesterday," Lavender explained. "If everybody likes them, I'll post the recipe on my Web site."

She strolled around the table and handed out muffins. Everyone seemed happy to have something else to eat.

"Mary-Kate," Lavender asked, holding out the tray, "would you like a muffin, too?"

Mary-Kate looked at the blueberry muffins and shook her head. "I don't think I can eat anything right now. I'm too worried."

Diary, I hope everything's all right. But just in case Mary-Kate needs a little support, I'm going with her to Mrs. Pritchard's office.

Because that's what sisters are for, right?

Dear Diary,

I was so scared waiting outside Mrs. Pritchard's office that I had goose bumps on top of my goose bumps!

"Deep breaths, Mary-Kate," Ashley whispered.

Ashley and I both sat on chairs facing Mrs. Pritchard's secretary, Joan Neilsen. The Head's door was shut—which made things even more scary!

"What if I did something horrible, Ashley?" I whispered. "What if it's so bad that Mrs. Pritchard asks Dad to come in?"

"You know you didn't do anything bad," Ashley whispered.

"But what if—"

"Think of the bright side," my sister tried. "Then we'll get a chance to see Dad!"

Our dad, Kevin Burke, is a college biology professor. His work takes him all over the world. Right now he's in charge of an important research project on woodpeckers in South Carolina.

Dad's job is way cooler than it sounds. I mean, how many kids can say that their dad's office is all the way up in a tree?

"Mary-Kate?" Mrs. Pritchard had opened her door and was looking straight at me. "You can come in now, Mary-Kate," she said. "You, too, Ashley."

My heart pounded as Ashley and I stood up.

"If they send me back home," I whispered, "you can have my school sweatshirts. And my portable TV. And my—"

"Mary-Kate!" Ashley whispered. "You're not going anywhere!"

We walked into Mrs. Pritchard's office. The Head was sitting with her hands folded on her desk. She was wearing a crisp white blouse with red pinstripes. Her light brown hair was parted on one side and fastened with a gold barrette.

"Hello, girls," Mrs. Pritchard said.

"Mrs. Pritchard, I'm sorry if I was hogging all the mustard packets!" I blurted out. "And if my gym locker stinks, I promise to clean it out right away!"

Mrs. Pritchard laughed. Then I heard someone else laugh. I looked to the side of the room and saw Mr. Patino, my history teacher.

What's he doing here? I wondered.

"This isn't about mustard packets or stinky gym lockers, Mary-Kate," Mrs. Pritchard said. "This is about the statewide history test all of you took yesterday morning."

Ashley and I exchanged glances.

"The history test?" I repeated.

My head began to spin. What if I failed? I'd never failed history before! What if Mr. Patino thought I

9

cheated? I would *never* think of cheating on a test!

"Congratulations, Mary-Kate," Mrs. Pritchard said. "You got one hundred percent on the test."

I stared at Mrs. Pritchard. *Did I hear her right?* I wondered. *Did Mrs. Pritchard just say I got 100 percent?*

"A-a-are you sure?" was all I could say.

Mr. Patino stepped forward. "I added up the scores myself, Mary-Kate," he said. "And you were the only student in the First Form who aced the test."

"No seventh grader has ever gotten one hundred percent on the statewide history test before," Mrs. Pritchard added.

"Really?" I couldn't believe it. I felt Ashley thump my back and say, "Congratulations!"

"I know how hard you studied, too," Mr. Patino said. "We're all very proud of you, Mary-Kate."

"That's why I'd like to have a special assembly next Tuesday at two-thirty in your honor," Mrs. Pritchard went on. "So I can present you with a certificate."

Now I *really* couldn't believe my ears. Special assemblies were always for special guests—like musicians, doctors, and White Oak graduates who became famous. And now Mrs. Pritchard wanted to have a special assembly for me!

"We'll name the assembly after you, too," Mr.

Patino told me. His dark eyes flashed. "We'll call it . . . the Mary-Kate Burke Special Assembly!"

"The Mary-Kate Burke Special Assembly!" Ashley exclaimed. "I like it! I like it!"

"You can invite guests," Mrs. Pritchard added. "Whomever you want."

The door swung open, and Mrs. Neilsen walked in. She handed me a piece of paper and said, "There you go. A photocopy of your famous test!"

"I want to keep the original copy in my files," Mr. Patino explained.

I looked down at the test. There it was, written in Mr. Patino's handwriting at the top of the paper: a big 100% with two exclamation points!

"How did *I* do on the test?" Ashley asked.

"The rest of the grades will be posted tomorrow," Mr. Patino said. "But if I remember, you did well, too, Ashley."

This time *I* thumped Ashley on the back.

"Well done, girls," Mrs. Pritchard said. "Now, why don't you go tell everyone the good news?"

Ashley and I turned and headed for the door.

"Oh, Mary-Kate?" Mrs. Pritchard said.

I spun around. "Yes, Mrs. Pritchard?"

"You can take as many mustard packets as you'd like," Mrs. Pritchard said. "But do clean out your gym locker as soon as possible."

"Yes, Mrs. Pritchard!" I said.

Ashley and I walked quietly out of the Head's office, but as soon as we were in the hall, we jumped up and down and shrieked!

"Wait until Dad finds out!" Ashley said. "He'll totally flip!"

"Maybe I'll invite Dad to the assembly next Tuesday," I said.

"Do you think he'll be able to come?" Ashley asked. "That woodpecker project he's working on is so important."

"It's worth a shot," I said.

Diary, is this totally amazing or what? My hours and hours of cramming finally paid off—big-time!

Chapter 2

Later Tuesday

Dear Diary,

My sister—a genius! Which started me thinking . . . everyone says that Mary-Kate and I look pretty much alike on the outside. We both have blond hair and blue eyes and practically the same smile. Maybe our brains are pretty much alike, too!

And guess what? Phoebe is going to write an article about Mary-Kate in the next issue of the White Oak *Acorn*.

We talked about it in the *Acorn* office today.

"I wish I could do something super special for Mary-Kate, too," I told Phoebe. "But I don't know what."

Phoebe spun around in her swivel chair. "I know!" she said. "Why don't you throw Mary-Kate a surprise party?"

"Because Mary-Kate is impossible to surprise," I said. "Remember?"

"Oh, yeah."

I leaned against a file cabinet and smiled. "Too bad I can't pretend the surprise party is for someone else," I said.

"Good idea." Phoebe chuckled. "Then she'd

never have a clue the party is really for her."

I stared at Phoebe. Then I pushed myself away from the file cabinet and said, "It *is* a great idea!"

"You mean pretend the party is for someone else?" Phoebe asked, standing up. "Don't you think Mary-Kate would figure it out sooner or later? When she sees us planning the party?"

"Unless . . ." I said slowly, "we get Mary-Kate to plan her own party!"

Phoebe's blue-framed glasses wiggled as she wrinkled her nose. "Now I *really* don't get it!" she said.

I paced the room as I explained. "It's like this," I said. "We ask Mary-Kate to pick out everything for a party we say is for someone else. Mary-Kate will have no clue that the party is for her."

"Oh, now I get it," Phoebe said, nodding. "Mary-Kate will choose all the stuff she loves, so she'll have the perfect party!"

"And most important—she'll be surprised!" I said. "She'll *finally* be surprised!"

Phoebe and I high-fived.

Then we got down to business.

"We'll tell all our friends the truth about the party," I said. "So they can be in on the surprise, too."

"What about Campbell?" Phoebe asked. "She's

14

Mary-Kate's roommate. What if she slips and accidentally tells Mary-Kate that the party is really for her?"

"Hmm," I said. "Mary-Kate says Campbell talks in her sleep, too."

We decided not to tell Campbell until the day of Mary-Kate's surprise party.

"Now," I said. "Who do we tell Mary-Kate the surprise party is for?"

"Good question," Phoebe said.

The door flew open. Lavender walked in carrying a green velvet tote bag. "I need to use a computer," Lavender said. "I'm writing an article about putting potpourri sachets in gym sneakers to keep them from smelling, and how to take bubble baths without a bathtub!"

Phoebe and I stared at Lavender as she sat down at the computer. Then we turned to each other and both whispered, "Lavender!"

"She's a good sport," I whispered.

"And she loves anything to do with parties," Phoebe whispered.

We ran over to Lavender.

"Lavender, we want to throw someone a party," I announced.

Lavender gave a little gasp. "You know I *love* planning parties. And I have the neatest idea for a party theme. It's called 'A Pirate's Chest Fest!'"

"No, Lavender—" I started to say.

"All you do is spread a bunch of pretty earrings, bracelets, and necklaces on a table," Lavender kept going.

"Lavender, wait—" I said again.

"Then you cover them all with clean, white sand," Lavender went on. "Then you tell everyone to dress up like pirates. When they get to the party, you give them each a little shovel and—"

"Lavender!" I shouted.

Lavender blinked. "What?"

"The party is for *you*!" I said.

"Me?" Lavender asked. "What are you talking about?"

I explained everything. When she understood that the party was for Mary-Kate and not for her, she smiled.

"I think it's a really great idea," Lavender said. "Mary-Kate will be planning her own party without even knowing it."

"Exactly!" Phoebe said.

"Mary-Kate will be surprised for the first time in her life," I added. "Will you go along with it, Lavender?"

"Sure," Lavender said. "I'll do it."

"Awesome!" I said. "I'll tell Mary-Kate about the

party tomorrow so she can start coming up with ideas."

"So, how about the pirate party?" Lavender asked. "Or a Wild West party with chili and line dancing?"

I smiled at Lavender. "Why don't we leave it to Mary-Kate?" I said. "I'm sure she'll pick out just the right stuff."

The three of us came up with a plan. We decided to have the party next Monday, the day before the special assembly. We would also try to get permission to have the party in the Student U.

"Let's invite some boys from Harrington, too," I added. "We definitely have to put Jordan on the list." Jordan Marshall is Mary-Kate's boyfriend.

"And Ross?" Phoebe teased.

"Of course!" I said with a grin, thinking of my boyfriend, Ross Lambert.

"Remember," I said. "We have to make everyone promise to keep this secret, or we'll never surprise Mary-Kate."

Dear Diary,

It has only been a few hours since I found out about my perfect score and already my whole life has changed!

Girls are coming up to me and congratulating

me—even girls I hardly know. Everyone seems so happy for me. Except snooty Dana Woletsky and her friends. All she had to say was, "What good are brains if nobody ever sees them?"

"Gee, Dana," I said. "I guess you'd need brains to answer that."

But here's the best part: I called Dad today!

I thought I'd chew off my fingernails waiting on the telephone line in my dorm, Porter House. I was right behind chatty Nora Banks and her mile-long telephone list. It seemed as if she were on the phone for hours, telling the entire world about her long-time crush on Toby Williams. Finally it was my turn to call Dad.

"You what?" Dad asked after I told him the news.

"I was the only student in the state of New Hampshire to ace the history test," I told him again.

I heard a loud "Woohoo!" He sounded like one of the birds he studies.

"Honey, I'm so proud of you!" Dad said. "I've always known my girls are brilliant."

"Mrs. Pritchard is going to have a special assembly for me next Tuesday afternoon at two-thirty," I said. "But I know you're busy watching woodpeckers, so it's okay if you can't make it."

"Who says I can't make it?" Dad said. "I wouldn't

miss your assembly for a whole tree of woodpeckers, Mary-Kate!"

"But I thought the project was important," I said.

"It is," Dad admitted. "But nothing is as important as you and Ashley."

I smiled. Dad coming to my assembly would
make it extra special.

"I'll fly to New Hampshire on Tuesday morning
in time for the assembly," Dad said. "I'll stay at the
nearby inn for a few days. The three of us can spend
some time together."

After saying good-bye, I hung up and ran to find
Ashley.

Wait until Ashley hears Dad is coming, I thought.
She'll be so happy!

The winter wind whipped my face as I ran across
campus. I tried hard to dart around the patches of
ice on the ground. Suddenly I felt someone grab my
arm. I twirled around and saw Jordan.

Jordan and I met in fencing class. We like a lot of
the same things—sports, rock music, and honey-
barbecued chicken. We also like each other. A lot!

"Congratulations!" Jordan said.

He pulled a shiny silver balloon from behind
his back. The letters on the balloon spelled out
SUPERSTAR!

Did I mention how sweet he is? I thanked Jordan.

Then I told him the good news about Dad coming to the assembly.

"That's great," Jordan said. "But before you go and tell Ashley, I kind of need a favor."

"Don't tell me," I joked. "You got bubble gum on the inside of your fencing mask and you need to borrow mine."

Jordan smiled and shook his head. "A guy in my dorm needs help," he explained. "His history teacher is giving a huge test next Tuesday morning. In order for him to keep playing football, he has to get his grade up."

"So he needs a tutor," I figured out.

"Not any tutor. The *best* tutor," Jordan said. "If this guy doesn't play on the Harrington team, our school is going to lose every game!"

"I've never tutored anyone before," I said. "Who is it?"

Jordan turned and shouted, "Lyle! Come and meet Mary-Kate!"

"Lyle?" I said in disbelief.

A group of Harrington boys were hanging out around a nearby bench. A tall boy with dark hair walked over. It was Lyle Wannamaker—one of the most popular guys at Harrington. And the quarterback of the football team!

"Did you say yes, Mary-Kate?" Lyle asked. He

pulled a piece of paper out of his pocket and handed it to me. "Check out the grade I got on my last history test. A sixty-five!"

I looked at Lyle's test. The teacher had written, "See me after class" at the bottom of the page.

"She totally graded this test unfairly. I know the Patriots fought for freedom during the Revolutionary War," Lyle said. "But they're also a football team. I should have gotten points for knowing that!"

Oh boy, Diary—if I tutor Lyle, we'll have a lot of work to do.

Jordan smiled at me.

I wanted to do Jordan a favor.

"Okay, Lyle," I said. "Why don't we meet tomorrow to study? After a few days of cramming, I'm sure you can bring up your grade."

Lyle pumped his fist in the air and shouted, "All right!"

"Thanks, Mary-Kate," Jordan said, giving my hand a squeeze. "If you help Lyle bring up his grade, you'll be saving him *and* the entire football team!"

"But no pressure!" Lyle added.

Right. No pressure at all.

My balloon fluttered in the wind as I carried it across campus.

Me, I thought. *A tutor?*

Diary, I always thought I wanted to be an actress or a rock singer when I grow up. But now I'm thinking that Professor Mary-Kate Burke has a nice ring to it. Don't you agree?

Chapter 3

Wednesday

Dear Diary,

Guess what? Dad is coming to visit next week—thanks to Mary-Kate and her special assembly!

There's a lot of stuff I want to do with Dad when he gets here, but first, I've got a party to plan. So this morning while Mary-Kate and I brushed our teeth, we talked about Dad, and Lyle Wannamaker, and I told her about Lavender's party.

"Lavender?" Mary-Kate said through a mouth full of toothpaste. "I thought her birthday is in the summer."

I glanced around the bathroom we share with a dozen other girls in Porter House. Our friends weren't there. Just two older girls who were drying their hair and putting on lip gloss.

"It's not a birthday party," I said as I rinsed my toothbrush under the faucet. "It's to celebrate the launch of Lavender's new Web site."

Mary-Kate rinsed and spit. "Lavender is great," she said. "But I never read her column."

"Why not?" I asked.

Mary-Kate stood back so I could see her outfit. She was wearing indigo jeans, a T-shirt with her favorite band's logo, and sneakers. "I mean, look at me, Ashley," she said. "Do I seem like the ribbons-and-lace type?"

"Not exactly," I admitted. It was true that Lavender's style is a little more traditional.

Mary-Kate screwed the cap on her toothpaste tube. It was time to ask her if she would help plan Lavender's party.

What if Mary-Kate says no? I wondered. *What if she can't help out with the party? What if she's too busy tutoring Lyle Wannamaker to help? Or too excited about her special assembly to think about someone else's party?*

"Mary-Kate," I said slowly. "This party is going to be a lot of work. . . ."

"I'll help," Mary-Kate said.

I stared at Mary-Kate. Did I get water in my ears during my shower? Did Mary-Kate just say she would help before I even asked her?

"Lavender is always doing nice things for us," Mary-Kate went on. "Like the time she sprayed Summer's stuffed animals with perfume to create a pretty scent in her new dorm room. And she sewed those curtains with the five layers of ruffles for Elise."

"And don't forget the blueberry muffins!" I added with a smile. "But are you sure you want to do it?"

"Sure," Mary-Kate said. "Remember that party I

put together for Grandma last summer? Where we all dressed up in nineteen-fifties clothes? It was so much fun!"

"It was," I agreed. "You're so good at putting together parties. Maybe you can think of the theme for Lavender's party."

"You mean be the party planner?" Mary-Kate asked. "That sounds like fun. We can go shopping."

I could have done a cartwheel right there. Not only did Mary-Kate want to help with the party, she wanted to pick out stuff, too. And I'd hardly had to ask!

"I'll make a list of things to buy," Mary-Kate said. "Party supplies. Food and music."

Diary, I am super psyched. All I have to do now is relax while Mary-Kate picks out all her favorite things. And she won't have a clue that the party is really for her!

Is my plan simply brilliant, or what?

Dear Diary,

Today was my first tutoring session with Lyle Wannamaker. And he's already learning. He now knows that Mount Rushmore is a historical landmark in South Dakota, not a roller-coaster park!

So you would think with my 100 percent history

score, the special assembly, Dad visiting next week, and all this cool attention, my life would be perfect, right?

WRONG.

Today my perfect world turned into the perfect *nightmare*!

It all started when Campbell Smith and I were hanging out in our room during midday break. Campbell was busy digging mud out of her cleats. I was taping the photocopy of my test right over my desk, where I would always see it.

There it is, I thought. *All the answers right!*

I ran my hand over the paper.

I still can't believe it!

I leaned over for a closer look.

I even got the last answer right, I thought. *The trickiest one of all!*

It was multiple choice: George Washington's presidential inauguration was held in: a) Philadelphia, b) Washington, D.C., c) Boston, d) New York City.

Most of the kids picked "b" but not me, I thought. *I picked New York City. I picked the letter . . . the letter . . .*

Hey . . . wait a minute!

I stared at the last question. The letter I wrote didn't look like a "d" at all! It looked like an "a"!

"Campbell!" I called. I jabbed my finger against

the paper. "What does this letter look like to you?"

Campbell dropped her cleat and walked over. She looked at the paper and said, "That's easy. It's an 'a.'"

My knees suddenly felt like Jell-O. I grabbed the desk to keep from sinking to the floor.

"Hey . . . wasn't the last answer supposed to be 'd'?" Campbell asked. "'New York City'?"

"Yes!" I wailed.

Campbell stared at me. Then she said, "Uh-oh!"

"If I wrote 'a' instead of 'd', it means I got the answer *wrong*!" I said. "And if I got the answer wrong, I didn't get one hundred percent on the test. I got ninety-eight percent. Which means I didn't set the state record!"

"Maybe Mr. Patino made a mistake."

I peeled the copy of the test off the wall. Then I held the paper up to the light, upside down, sideways—every single way. But whichever way I looked at it, the answer was still wrong!

"How can Mr. Patino make a mistake?" I cried. "He's a teacher! Teachers aren't supposed to make mistakes!"

"This teacher did," Campbell said. "Now that you know about the goof-up, I guess you have to tell someone about it."

I turned and stared at Campbell. "But the big

assembly is in just a few days! Mrs. Pritchard has announced it to Harrington and the school board. And my dad already planned to fly in just for the assembly!"

"Then what are you going to do?" Campbell asked.

"I don't have a clue!" I said, then I calmed down a bit. "I'll figure it out. Just do me a favor, Campbell. Don't tell anyone about this until I break the news to Mrs. Pritchard and Mr. Patino!"

She agreed. She's the best roommate.

But what should I do, Diary?

Do I tell Mrs. Pritchard about the mistake so she can call off the special assembly?

Thursday

Dear Diary,

Yesterday was the worst day of my life! Everywhere I went I felt like everyone knew that I didn't really ace the history test!

I couldn't even look at my friends—or Ashley. She was so proud of me!

I knew immediately what I had to do. I decided to tell Mrs. Pritchard the truth about the test first thing this morning so she could call off the special assembly.

"Mrs. Pritchard will see you now, Mary-Kate," Mrs. Neilsen said.

I stood up and walked into Mrs. Pritchard's office. She looked extra cheerful today with her bright pink sweater and even brighter smile.

"Well, Mary-Kate," Mrs. Pritchard said from behind her desk. "Aren't you the early bird?"

My heart was pounding inside my chest. I wanted to turn around and run out of the office. Even though I had done nothing wrong, I didn't like to disappoint anyone.

I took a deep breath and said, "Mrs. Pritchard, there's something you need to know. We really shouldn't be having a special assembly—"

"Oh, Mary-Kate," Mrs. Pritchard chuckled. "You studied hard and got one hundred percent on a statewide history test. If that isn't reason for a special assembly, I don't know what is!"

"But—"

"This is a really big moment for White Oak Academy, too," Mrs. Pritchard went on. "And for Mr. Patino."

"Mr. Patino?" I said.

"He taught the student who got one hundred percent!" Mrs. Pritchard explained. "That's why I'm going to give him a special award, too."

"An award?" I gulped. "What kind of an award?"

"A Teacher of the Year award!" Mrs. Pritchard declared. "What do you think of *that*, Mary-Kate?"

My head was spinning too fast to think. All I knew was that this assembly wasn't just about me anymore. It was about Mr. Patino, too! "That's . . . great," I squeaked.

"I thought you'd be pleased, Mary-Kate," Mrs. Pritchard said. She folded her hands on her desk and asked, "Now, was there anything else you wanted to tell me?"

My tongue felt as dry as day-old cotton candy. I opened my mouth and tried to speak, but nothing came out.

Candles, Cake, Celebrate!

"Well, then," Mrs. Pritchard said. "I'd better call the audiovisual department. I want them to project your test on a big screen in the auditorium, so everyone can see it."

So everyone can see I got the last answer wrong! I thought.

"Thank you, Mrs. Pritchard," I mumbled. "I'd better go to my first class now."

I left the Head's office and walked across campus like a zombie. I hardly heard Campbell call my name.

"So?" Campbell asked, running over. "Did you tell Mrs. Pritchard?"

"Nope," I said, embarrassed.

Campbell looked confused. "Then you're going to tell Mr. Patino first, right?" she asked.

"Nope," I said again. I hadn't done anything wrong. So why was I feeling so bad?

"How come?" Campbell asked.

"Because," I said. "How can I tell the new *Teacher of the Year* that he made a mistake?"

Dear Diary,

The minute I woke up today I couldn't wait to tell our friends about Mary-Kate's surprise party. Our first-period gym class was the perfect time. Mary-Kate

31

was excused to talk to Mrs. Pritchard about something, so she wouldn't be around.

"What do you think of my idea?" I asked after I went over the whole plan.

My friends and I sat on the bleachers. We were tying our sneakers and waiting for Ms. Phillips, the gym teacher, to blow her whistle.

"Let me get this straight," Cheryl said. "You want us to pretend we're giving a surprise party for Lavender when we're really giving it for Mary-Kate?"

"And Mary-Kate is going to plan the party?" Wendy Linden asked. "Not knowing that the party is for her?"

"Right!" I said. "It's the only way I'm going to finally surprise Mary-Kate. You saw how hard it is to surprise her."

Cheryl turned to Lavender. She was pulling potpourri sachets out of her sneakers.

"What do you think, Lavender?" Cheryl asked. "Won't it be hard to pretend you don't know about the party?"

"The hardest part will be not *planning* this party," Lavender said. "You all know how much I love to plan parties."

I jumped off the bleachers and faced my friends. "What do you say?" I asked. "Are you all in?"

Candles, Cake, Celebrate!

Cheryl, Elise, and Wendy looked at one another. Then they each nodded and smiled.

"Anything for another party!" Summer said.

"We haven't had a party in over two weeks!" Elise said with a wink. "That was ages ago!"

We talked about the party as we walked toward the volleyball net. I also told them about my dad coming for the assembly. I was so excited to see him; it had been a while since our last school break. But suddenly it seemed like I had a lot to do to get ready.

"What are you going to do first?" Cheryl asked.

"Tomorrow after school I'm taking Mary-Kate to town," I said. "For a little party supply shopping spree. Knowing Mary-Kate, she'll pick out the coolest things."

"Like inflatable guitars!" Wendy said.

"And jumbo sunglasses!" Phoebe said.

"And glow-in-the-dark headbands!" Cheryl added.

"And glitter!" Elise said. She gave a thumbs-up sign. "Lots of glitter to pour on everything!"

"Okay, okay." I laughed. "But I need you all to promise that you won't tell Mary-Kate about our plan."

Everyone promised just as the sound of Ms. Phillips's whistle made me jump.

Two of a Kind Diaries

"Okay, girls!" Ms. Phillips called. "Let's play volleyball!"

I practically skipped to the volleyball net—that's how happy I was. Now that all of our friends know about the party, it's official: I'm finally going to surprise Mary-Kate!

Chapter 5

Friday

Dear Diary,

Of all classes, I had to have history first today!

"How can I sit in Mr. Patino's class knowing what I know?" I asked Campbell as we got dressed this morning. "I am so dreading this."

"Yeah, I can tell," Campbell said as she pulled on her sweatshirt.

"How?" I asked.

Campbell nodded down at my feet. "You're so distracted, you put on two different-colored socks!" she said.

I stared down at my feet. "Okay." I sighed. "Time to get a grip."

I kicked off my shoes and socks and rummaged through my drawer until I found a matching pair. Then Campbell and I put on our jackets, hats, and scarves and rushed out of Porter House. We were already late for breakfast.

"I can't believe I'm the only one who knows about this," Campbell said as we headed toward the dining room. "And I can't believe you didn't tell Ashley yet. She's your sister!"

I shook my head. "Ashley is counting the days

until our dad comes for the assembly," I said. "How can I tell her there won't be an assembly—or a visit from Dad?"

As we walked, I hardly noticed the other kids rushing around in the winter cold. All I could think about was seeing Mr. Patino in my history class later. "Maybe Mr. Patino won't be in today," I said. "Maybe we'll have a sub."

Campbell stopped walking. I stopped, too.

"This is nuts, Mary-Kate," Campbell said firmly. "You're acting like you did something wrong. And you didn't."

"What do *you* think I should do?" I asked.

"Get real with Mr. Patino," Campbell said. "Tell him about the grade, then let *him* decide whether to tell Mrs. Pritchard or not. It's not *your* fault that he made a mistake grading your test."

I know, I thought. *Campbell is right. I didn't do anything wrong!* "Thanks, Campbell!" I spun around and began walking the other way.

"Where are you going?" Campbell called. "What about breakfast?"

"Save me a corn muffin!" I called back. "I want to catch Mr. Patino before class starts."

I hurried inside the history building and went straight to my classroom.

I pushed open the door and peeked inside. Mr.

Patino was sitting at his desk, shuffling through a stack of papers. He was wearing charcoal gray pants and a dark green V-neck sweater.

"Excuse me, Mr. Patino," I said.

Mr. Patino looked up at me and grinned as I walked into the room. "Mary-Kate!" he said. "I was just grading some history essays."

"I don't want to interrupt," I said quickly. "You might goof—um . . . I mean not finish them in time for class!"

"Come on in," Mr. Patino said cheerfully. "There's always time for the history champ!"

Some history champ, I thought as I stepped inside. *Wait until he finds out the truth!*

"Mrs. Pritchard told me about my Teacher of the Year award yesterday," Mr. Patino said. "It's the biggest honor I've had since I started teaching!"

"Really?" I gulped.

"And it's all because of you, Mary-Kate," Mr. Patino said. "Your acing that test let me know that I'm doing my job. That means so much to me."

Wow! I thought. He was really being honest about himself with me. It was weird to talk to a teacher like this, I realized.

I opened my mouth to speak, but Mr. Patino beat me to it.

"Did you know that my whole family is coming

to see me get the award?" Mr. Patino asked. "Even my mom!"

"Your mom?" I squeaked.

"She's coming in all the way from Boston," Mr. Patino said. Now he looked a little embarrassed. "She's dragging along my aunt Josephine, my uncle Sal, my cousin Donna . . . "

His whole family is coming, I thought. *I can't disappoint Mr. Patino and his family.*

"So," Mr. Patino said. He leaned back in his chair and smiled. "What's on your mind, Mary-Kate?"

"Um," I said. "I just wanted to say . . . "

"Yes?" Mr. Patino asked.

The door flew open. A few early students began filing into the classroom. There was no way could I tell him now!

"I just wanted to say congratulations!" I blurted out. "On your award!"

"Well, thanks, Mary-Kate," Mr. Patino said. "Or should I say . . . Champ!"

As I walked to my desk I realized that maybe the right thing to do wasn't necessarily right.

I'd better keep my mouth shut, I thought. *And pretend to the whole school that nothing is wrong!*

I would straighten it all out after the assembly. Mrs. Pritchard would understand. She had to. I was sure of it.

Candles, Cake, Celebrate!

Diary, it's a good thing I'm in the drama department. Because this is going to be the hardest acting job of my life!

Dear Diary,

Ready . . . set . . . shop!

That's what I told Mary-Kate as we hopped aboard the White Oak Shuttle Van to town. As we sat on the lumpy seats I couldn't stop talking about the party—or about Dad!

"Maybe we can take Dad to that new burger place in town," I said. "You know, where they have thirty different kinds of burgers?"

My sister stared out of the window.

"Earth to Mary-Kate," I said into her ear.

Mary-Kate snapped out of her trance and said, "What?"

"You look so serious," I said. "What's up?"

"I was just thinking about . . . Lavender's party!" Mary-Kate said, cracking a smile. "And all the neat stuff we can get for it!"

The van stopped in town, and we climbed out. We headed straight over to Party Hearty, on Main Street.

Once we were inside I grabbed a shopping cart. Mary-Kate walked next to me as I pushed it down Aisle #1. The first thing I spotted was a shelf full of

Hollywood-style party supplies. There were movie clapboards, black-and-silver top hats, and huge gold cardboard stars!

Perfect! I thought. *Mary-Kate loves acting and the movies!* "Let's grab a couple of these," I said, taking a pair of jumbo sunglasses.

"Let's not," Mary-Kate said. She snatched the sunglasses and put them back on the shelf.

"What are you doing?" I asked.

"This stuff is wrong for this party," Mary-Kate said. "Lavender isn't about Hollywood glam and glitz. Let's keep moving."

Okay, so it won't be a Hollywood party, I thought as I pushed the cart. *There's a ton of other fun stuff in this place.*

We walked down Aisle #2. Sitting on a shelf was a giant rubber cowboy hat. "Yee-haa!" I said, popping it onto my head. "This is fun!"

But Mary-Kate pulled it right off my head and said, "Fun for us, not for Lavender. She'll think it's tacky."

I watched as Mary-Kate placed the cowboy hat back on the shelf. "So what do you think we should pick?" I asked.

"Follow me," Mary-Kate said.

She led me to Aisle #5. I froze as I looked around. The shelves were stocked with frilly parasols, lacy-

40

looking paper plates, and baskets filled with dried and silk flowers!

Uh-oh! I thought. *Mary-Kate can't have a frilly party like this. It's not her style. I've got to stop her!*

Mary-Kate smiled as she picked up a flower basket. "Lavender will love this!" she exclaimed.

I yanked it out of her hand and put it back. "Too cute," I said.

"Then what about these?" Mary-Kate asked. She held up a package of heart-shaped doilies.

"Too precious," I said, putting it back.

Mary-Kate planted her hands on her hips and said, "Ashley! What are you doing?"

"Maybe all this stuff is a little too sweet," I said carefully. "Just looking at it is giving me cavities."

Mary-Kate tossed a paper tablecloth into the cart—a tablecloth decorated with pink flowers! "I know what I'm doing, Ashley," Mary-Kate said. "And you did make me Lavender's party planner, right?"

I nodded slowly.

"Okay, then," Mary-Kate said. She took over the cart and began to push it. "Where can we find some pink plastic teacups?"

Pink plastic teacups? Lace doilies? Parasols? This isn't a party for Mary-Kate. It's a perfect party . . . for Lavender!

Two of a Kind Diaries

As we rode back in the van with bags of pretty party supplies, I had the most horrible thought . . . .

What if my brilliant idea of letting Mary-Kate plan her own party wasn't so brilliant at all?

What if it was a *big mistake*?

Chapter 6

Saturday

Dear Diary,

Saturday mornings are usually pretty lazy at White Oak. But this Saturday morning was the total opposite!

After breakfast I met Phoebe and Lavender in the *Acorn* office. Phoebe was busy writing her article about Mary-Kate. Lavender was busy finishing her latest column. And I was busy complaining about my disastrous shopping spree with Mary-Kate. . . .

"First she picked out ruffled parasols!" I cried. "Then she grabbed a bunch of heart-shaped cookie cutters!"

"Fun!" Lavender exclaimed. "I love ruffled parasols. And heart-shaped cookies."

"But this party isn't for you, Lavender," I reminded her. "It's for Mary-Kate!"

Phoebe turned around from her computer and asked, "Didn't you try to make Mary-Kate go for the stuff she likes?"

"Yes, but it didn't work," I said. "Mary-Kate even ditched a neat giant rubber cowboy hat. She said it was—"

"Tacky?" Lavender cut in.

"Exactly," I admitted. "In the end, Mary-Kate

picked out great stuff for you, Lavender, but not for herself."

"Why don't you just tell Mary-Kate that you don't need her help anymore?" Phoebe asked.

"And hurt her feelings?" I gasped.

"You won't if you do it nicely," Lavender said. "I once wrote a column called 'Ditching with Kindness.' I can print it out, if you'd like!"

The door swung open, and Mary-Kate walked in. "Hi, guys," Mary-Kate said. She started to say something more, then stopped, looking straight at Lavender. She was carrying a brown folder under her arm.

She probably wants to talk to us about the party! I realized.

"Um . . . Lavender?" I said. "Weren't you going to show Wendy how to put together a scrapbook?"

"Scrapbook?" Lavender asked.

I tilted my head toward the door.

"Oh, the scrapbook!" Lavender said. She saved her computer file and jumped up. "Thanks for reminding me!"

Lavender gave a little wave as she left the office.

"I thought I'd find you guys in here," Mary-Kate said. "What are you working on?"

Uh-oh! I had to think fast.

"Your article!" Phoebe said, standing up. "Wait

until you see what I'm writing, Mary-Kate. You're going to love it!"

Mary-Kate's smile turned into a frown.

"Are you sure you want to write about me?" Mary-Kate asked. "So I aced a history test. Big deal."

"You were the only student in the state who aced the history test," I said. "It's a huge deal!"

"You earned this article, Mary-Kate," Phoebe said. "And the special assembly. And the par—"

I gave Phoebe a quick jab with my elbow.

"Ow!" Phoebe cried. "I mean—wow! This article is going to be good!"

Mary-Kate began opening the brown folder. "I was thinking about food for Lavender's party," she said. "And I came up with some really cool ideas."

"Like what?" I asked. "Pizza? Guacamole dip? Mini-franks wrapped in dough?"

Those were Mary-Kate's favorite party foods. But she shook her head and said, "More like little cucumber sandwiches and three-bean salad."

"What are those?" I asked.

"They're the types of foods Lavender wrote about in her columns," Mary-Kate said. She pulled out some papers and handed them to Phoebe and me. "One time she wrote about watercress sandwiches with the crusts cut off."

"Watercress?" Phoebe asked. "You mean that green stuff that looks like soggy grass? And tastes like it, too?"

"Mary-Kate, that sounds totally gross!" I complained.

"I know," Mary-Kate admitted. "But Lavender likes it. And it is her party!"

"What about onion rings?" I asked. "And honey-barbecued chicken?"

"Yeah, right!" Mary-Kate said and laughed. "As if Lavender would ever eat with her hands!"

"But—" I started to say.

"I almost forgot!" Mary-Kate said. "I have to buy purple food coloring for the white bread."

I was afraid to ask. But I did . . . "You're dying the bread . . . purple?" I asked.

"Not purple, silly—lavender!" Mary-Kate said, her eyes gleaming. "Get it?"

Mary-Kate stuffed the papers back into her folder. Phoebe shot me a look. A look that said, *"What are you waiting for?"*

"Mary-Kate!" I blurted out.

"What?" Mary-Kate said.

"Why don't you let me take over the party planning now?" I asked.

"Why?" Mary-Kate asked.

"You're going to be busy tutoring Lyle," I said.

"And getting ready for the special assembly this Tuesday."

"What's to get ready?" Mary-Kate asked. "Besides, I'm having fun."

Mary-Kate turned to leave. I quickly grabbed her arm.

"What?" Mary-Kate asked.

"Why should you have all the fun?" I asked with a chuckle. "Why don't you let me do something for a change?"

"Yeah, Mary-Kate!" Phoebe agreed. "I'm sure you could find something for Ashley to do."

Like exchange the party supplies? I thought hopefully. *Or cook barbecued chicken and onion rings?*

"Okay," Mary-Kate said. "You can print out the invitations on your computer."

"Invitations!" I said. "You got it!"

"But don't forget to use the lavender paper I bought," Mary-Kate ordered. "And spray each piece of paper with perfume."

"Perfume?" I said.

"The sweeter the better!" Mary-Kate said. "And don't lick the envelopes. Use lavender sealing wax instead."

"Sealing wax?" I cried.

Phoebe and I stared at Mary-Kate as she left the office.

"You're right," Phoebe said. "She's out of control."

Diary, getting Mary-Kate to plan this party was easy. Getting her to stop planning this party is almost *impossible*!

Dear Diary,

So far so good. Nobody seems to have a clue that Mr. Patino botched up my history test. Not even Ashley. But that doesn't make things easier. I keep telling myself that as soon as the assembly is over, I can explain it all to Mrs. Pritchard.

But Mary-Kate Mania is still sweeping the school. Like that dumb article Phoebe is writing about me in the *Acorn*!

"I have to stop Phoebe from writing that article, Campbell," I told my roomie in the Student U.

"How come?" Campbell asked. "Don't you want to see your name in print?"

Campbell and I were sitting in beanbag chairs, sipping hot cocoa with marshmallows.

"I can't have the whole First Form reading that I'm the history champ when I'm really not," I said. "And I have to stop tutoring Lyle, too."

"But you're still good in history," Campbell said.

"Not good enough to ace the statewide history

test," I said in a low voice. "And Lyle still thinks he's getting the real deal."

"Are you going to tell him about Mr. Patino's mistake?" Campbell asked.

I shook my head. "I have to make up an excuse," I said. "Like I have no time to tutor him or something like that."

"Speaking of time," Campbell said, and pointed to the clock on the wall. "Aren't you supposed to meet Lyle in the library in ten minutes?"

I nodded, sipped my last drop of cocoa, and tossed the paper cup in the trashcan. Then I grabbed my jacket and my history books. "Wish me luck, Campbell," I said.

I ran across campus to the library. Once inside I scanned the room. The tables were filled with studying students from White Oak and Harrington. Lyle was there, too. He was wearing a football jersey and a backwards cap.

"Yo, Mary-Kate!" Lyle called. He waved at me with his history book. "Over here!"

Mrs. Nagel, one of the librarians, was sitting behind her desk and frowning. She hates loud voices in the library.

"Hi, Lyle," I whispered, sitting down next to him. "I hate to tell you this, but I have bad news."

"The Jets lost the game?" Lyle asked.

"No," I said. "I can't tutor you anymore, Lyle. I just don't have enough time."

Lyle's eyes popped wide open. "But you have to tutor me!" he said. "I told practically everyone that you're going to help me pass the big history test on Tuesday."

"I know, but—" I started to say.

"The whole school is rooting for me!" Lyle cut in. "And they're counting on *you* to keep me on the team!"

"Great," I muttered.

"If anyone can help me pass the test, it's you, Mary-Kate," Lyle said. "You're the champ!"

There it was again. The "C" word!

Lyle will not let me quit, I thought. *So what if I try to make Lyle quit instead?*

I looked at Lyle and said, "Okay, Lyle. I'll keep tutoring you."

"All riiight!" Lyle cheered. He thumped my shoulder. "You're the best, Mary-Kate!"

"The best?" I asked, narrowing my eyes. "Did you just say the best?"

"Yeah, why?" Lyle asked.

I stood up and planted my hands on my hips. "Nice try, Wannamaker!" I said. "But if you think you're going to ace this test by buttering me up, think again!"

Candles, Cake, Celebrate!

Lyle stood up, looked down at me, and said, "Huh?"

"From now on I want you reading three chapters a night instead of two!" I said. "Then I want you to reread them each morning and memorize every single fact—until you have American history oozing out of your ears!"

"Three chapters?" Lyle gulped.

"The whole nine yards!" I exclaimed. "Got a problem with that, Wannamaker?"

Lyle shook his head slowly.

"Good!" I said. "Now go out there and crack those chapters. And be here tomorrow at ten A.M. sharp!"

"Tomorrow?" Lyle asked. "But tomorrow's Sunday. The team and I were going to practice our passes."

"Would you rather pass a football—or this test?" I stood up and pointed to the door. "Now go, go, go, go, go!"

Lyle jumped up, grabbed his books, and darted out of the door.

That ought to do it, I thought with a grin.

But when I turned around, I gulped. All of the kids in the library were staring at me!

"Um—he had to leave suddenly!" I said.

"And you have to leave, too, young lady," Mrs.

Nagel called from her desk. "There will be no shouting in the library at any time!"

"Sorry!" I squeaked.

As I rushed out of the library I was sure Lyle was going to be busy looking for a history tutor. And this time, Diary, it wouldn't be me!

Chapter 7

Sunday

Dear Diary,

I can't believe the party is tomor-  row. Which means if I'm going to take over Mary-Kate's surprise party, it will have to be *today*!

And that means firing Mary-Kate!

"What do you think of my plan, you guys?" I asked.

I scooped up a heap of snow between my gloves. It had snowed all night. So this morning the whole school ran outside to have some serious winter fun—sledding and snowboarding. My friends and I were building a snowman.

"I'm not sure, Ashley," Elise said. "We might hurt Mary-Kate's feelings."

"We'll only be hurting Mary-Kate's feelings for now," I explained. "But the party is tomorrow night. And the minute we yell 'surprise', she'll forget all about it."

"Okay," Summer said. She wrapped her scarf tighter around her neck. "But I'm usually not this mean."

"You're *never* mean, Summer!" Cheryl chuckled.

As I slapped a chunk of snow onto the snowman's shoulder, I saw Mary-Kate trudging toward us. In her hand was a big brown shopping bag.

"I wonder what's in the bag," Elise whispered.

"Forget about the bag," I said. "Just remember what I told you to say."

Mary-Kate stopped a few feet away from us. She tilted her head as she checked out the snowman. "Cool snowman," she said. Then she reached into the shopping bag. "Ta-daaa!" she said. "Look what I found in the theater department!"

I stared at the flower garland that Mary-Kate pulled out.

"The Fourth Form used them in their play *A Midsummer Night's Dream*," Mary-Kate said, putting it on. "I thought we could each wear one at Lavender's party."

My friends exchanged uneasy glances. Phoebe was the first to speak up.

"Mary-Kate," Phoebe said. "Your ideas for Lavender's party kind of . . . kind of . . . "

"What?" Mary-Kate asked.

"Reek!" Cheryl blurted out.

"Yeah," Wendy piped in. "The decorations you picked out look like something from *Little House on the Prairie*."

"And stuff like watercress," Elise said, "should be served to cows, not people!"

"And that garland!" Summer said. "If we all wear those, we'll look like flower fairies!"

Mary-Kate stared at us, stunned.

"They're right, Mary-Kate," I said. "This frilly stuff isn't cutting it."

"I don't think this party-planner thing is working," Cheryl said.

I hate this! I thought. *I hate upsetting Mary-Kate— even if it is just for now!*

But I knew it was for Mary-Kate's own good. And for the good of her surprise party!

"Well . . . " Mary-Kate said slowly. "If you really feel that way—"

"Ooooh!" a voice cried. "Beautiful!"

Everyone spun around. Lavender was walking through the snow toward us. She was wearing a winter-white coat, a white furry hat, and pink leather gloves.

"That garland is gorgeous!" Lavender exclaimed. "And what a great way to add color in the winter. I'm going to write that up in my next column!"

I stared at Lavender. What was she doing? She was supposed to discourage Mary-Kate from picking out this kind of stuff!

"You like it?" Mary-Kate asked Lavender.

"I *love* it!" Lavender said. "I didn't know you have such awesome taste, Mary-Kate!"

Lavender gave a little wave and began walking away.

Mary-Kate turned to us and smiled. "You were saying?" she asked.

Silence.

"Okay, then," Mary-Kate said. "Let's decorate the U tonight for Lavender's party. See you there."

Mary-Kate began walking toward Porter House. Lavender was walking the other way.

"I'll be right back," I said.

It wasn't easy catching up to Lavender in the show, but I finally did.

"Hi, Ashley," Lavender said. "What's up?"

"Lavender, what were you thinking?" I asked. "Mary-Kate isn't supposed to pick the kind of stuff you like!"

Lavender looked surprised. "I thought *everybody* likes flowers," she said. "I mean, what's not to like?"

I stared at Lavender as she kept on walking.

Some help she's turning out to be! I thought.

Especially since Mary-Kate's party is *tomorrow*!

Dear Diary,

Do you believe I almost got booted off of Lavender's secret surprise party?

Candles, Cake, Celebrate!

After picking out some more garlands for Lavender's party, I had to go to the library to return some books. I knew Lyle wouldn't be there. No way would he want General Mary-Kate Burke tutoring him again!

Until I walked into the library and heard, "Yo! Mary-Kate, over here!"

No, I thought. *It can't be.*

I turned my head. It was. It was Lyle Wannamaker sitting at his usual table with a big grin on his face!

"Lyle!" I whispered as I walked over. "What are you doing here?"

"You're kidding, right?" Lyle asked. "We're supposed to cram for the history test. Remember?"

I placed my books on the table. "You still want me to tutor you?" I asked. "Even though I was practically a pit bull yesterday?"

Lyle nodded. "You reminded me of my football coach," Lyle said. "He's a tyrant, but we win almost every game!"

I groaned under my breath. My plan was backfiring.

Big-time!

"I hope you don't mind helping out a few of my friends, too," Lyle added.

"What do you mean 'a few friends'?" I asked.

"Yo, guys!" Lyle called. "Come meet the teach!"

About six guys, each with broad shoulders, turned around from the magazine rack. Four of them were wearing football jerseys. And most of them were almost six feet tall!

"Meet my teammates," Lyle explained as they walked over. "They need to boost their grades, too."

"And we have only two days to do it!" a guy with a buzz cut said.

"So what do you want *me* to do?" I asked.

"I thought we could all cram together," Lyle said. "You know, like a study group."

"You mean a study *team*!" another guy grunted.

This is unreal, I thought. *Not only am I still tutoring Lyle, now I'm tutoring the whole Harrington football team!* "Okay," I said with a sigh. "Let's study."

"Mary-Kate! Mary-Kate! Mary-Kate!" the guys grunted.

I almost fell over as they thumped my back. There was no way out now. I had to tutor Lyle and his team.

Chapter 8

Later Sunday

Dear Diary,

Lucky for us, Mrs. Pritchard gave us permission to take over the Student U for Mary-Kate's surprise party. Not so lucky is that Mary-Kate is still the Major Party Planner. . . .

"I checked with the dining room staff earlier," Mary-Kate told us. "They're starting to prepare the party food today."

I listened to my sister as I blew up a lavender-colored, heart-shaped balloon. The others were hanging up crepe paper, spreading out tablecloths, and laying out the dainty lacy doilies.

There was nothing more we could do to stop Mary-Kate from planning her own party. We just had to deal with it!

"Wait until you hear the tunes I picked out for the party," Mary-Kate said.

"Rock music?" I asked.

Mary-Kate loves rock more than anything. For sure, she'd want to play rock music at Lavender's party!

"Not exactly," Mary-Kate said. She passed a bunch of CDs around the room. "Check it out."

We wrinkled our noses as we read the cases.

"*Tranquil Breezes*?" I asked.

"*Gentle Falling Leaves*?" Elise read.

"*Smoldering Volcanoes*?" Cheryl asked.

"Volcanoes are rocks," Summer joked. "Maybe this *is* rock music!"

"Not a chance!" I said, turning to my sister. "Mary-Kate, what kind of music is this?"

"It's Lavender's type of music," Mary-Kate explained. "I'll play it for you." Mary-Kate carried a CD to the boom box.

"Here we go again," I muttered to Elise. "Now Mary-Kate is picking out the wrong kind of music!"

"*Shh*," Elise whispered. "Maybe it's not so bad."

Mary-Kate slipped a CD in the box. She clicked the PLAY button. In a few seconds the Student U was filled with the soft sounds of harps and violins.

"I heard this song before," Wendy giggled. "In an elevator!"

"Hey, some people like this stuff," Mary-Kate said as she stacked the CDs on a table.

Some people, I thought. *But not Mary-Kate!*

"It's kind of nice," Summer said. She started swaying her hips. "But how do you dance to it?"

"Like this!" Mary-Kate said. She grabbed a long piece of crepe paper. Then she waved it in the air as she twirled around the room. "Feel the music. And be one with nature!"

Everyone giggled as Mary-Kate glided around the room. It was kind of funny, even though we had to get back on track. I wished Phoebe were there. But Phoebe was in the *Acorn* office working on her article about Mary-Kate.

I have to take control of this party disaster, I thought. *But how?*

"Can we please switch the music?" Cheryl groaned. "Before it puts us all to sleep?"

"Switch the music"? Did she say "switch the music"?

I glanced over at the stack of CDs on the table.

That's it, I thought. *Switching the CDs would be a snap!*

Maybe there *are* some things I can do!

I could start stocking up on Mary-Kate's favorite rock music today. And so what about the other food? I can still order a cake with her favorite chocolate frosting! I could ask the bakery to write "Way to Go, Mary-Kate!" on the top. And cover the cake with fifty candles—one for each answer she got right!

It'll be hard to keep a secret from her, with all the work I'll have to do, but it will be worth it.

Can this party be saved, Diary?

Two of a Kind Diaries

Dear Diary,

There I was, standing on a ladder and hanging lavender streamers from the ceiling, when I noticed someone was missing. "Where's Phoebe?" I asked.

"In the *Acorn's* office," Wendy said. "She's still working on that article about you."

"What?" I gasped.

Oh, no! I thought. *I was so busy with the party, I forgot about Phoebe's article!*

"Be right back," I said.

Everyone eyeballed me as I climbed down from the ladder and ran out of the Student U.

I have to stop Phoebe! I thought as I raced toward the *Acorn's* office. *I can't have the whole school reading that I'm the history champ when I never was!*

I skidded around the corner and slammed right into Phoebe! Papers flew out of her hands and scattered on the floor.

"What's the rush, Mary-Kate?" Phoebe asked.

I picked up the papers and began to babble. "Phoebe, did you know that Ellen Marks just won the school-wide science fair? And that Gillian Guberman has been asked to paint a mural in the gym locker room? And did you know that Cecily Olivieri never gets Novocain when she goes to the dentist? She uses her mind to control her pain!"

"And you're telling me all of this because . . . ?" Phoebe asked patiently.

"Because that's cutting-edge news!" I declared. "I won't be insulted if you decide to write about them and not me!"

"Too late!" Phoebe said. She took the papers from me and smiled. "Your article is being printed as we speak."

"It is?" I gulped.

"Here's a mock-up of the front page," Phoebe said. She held up a sheet of paper. Splashed across the top was the headline: "First Form History Whiz Aces Statewide Test!"

"Oh," was all I could say.

As I stared at the headline I had the sudden urge to tell Phoebe the truth about Mr. Patino's goof-up.

Phoebe is sensible and level-headed. Maybe she'll know what I should do, I thought.

"Phoebe," I said. "Mr. Patino—"

"Mr. Patino!" Phoebe interrupted. "I almost forgot!"

"Forgot what?" I asked.

"Ta-daa!" Phoebe sang. She held up another paper.

This one had an article and a photograph of Mr. Patino on it!

"I interviewed Mr. Patino for the *Acorn*!" Phoebe

said proudly. "And it's one of the best articles I've ever written."

"R-r-really?" I stammered.

Come to think of it, maybe I won't tell Phoebe about Mr. Patino's mistake, I thought.

"The issue will come out Tuesday, the day of the special assembly," Phoebe told me. "But I'd better get these articles to Mrs. Pritchard's office. She likes to read them before they go out."

I watched Phoebe hurry down the hall.

Phoebe is totally psyched about this award, too, I thought. *Now I know I'm doing the right thing by not telling anyone about Mr. Patino's mistake!*

But if doing the right thing is supposed to make you feel good, then why do I feel so *awful*?

Chapter 9

Monday, PARTY DAY

Dear Diary,

I feel way better now.

Dad is coming in tomorrow for the special assembly. And I've been able to add a few personal touches to Mary-Kate's surprise party tonight.

Starting with the party music . . .

"Thanks for meeting me here, Ross," I told my boyfriend during midday break. "But I thought you were bringing your CD collection."

The two of us were walking toward the Student U together. Ross looked really cute today in his black pants and gray sweater.

"I have something better than CDs," Ross said.

I stopped in front of the Student U and stared at him. "What do you mean, Ross?" I asked. "I need rock music for Mary-Kate's surprise party. And I need it now!"

"Don't worry, Ashley," Ross said chuckling. He opened the door of the U, and we stepped inside.

"Whoa!" Ross said as he stared at the frilly tablecloth, dried-flower baskets, and hanging parasols. "This place has more lace than my grandmother's living room!"

"I know, I know," I said. "Now please go back to your dorm and bring me your CD collection. I need Gag Reflex, the Sonic Puppies—"

"And Toe Jam!" a boy's voice cut in. "They really rock!"

I whirled around. A guy wearing a leather jacket, jeans, and black sunglasses walked in. He looked around and gave a long whistle. "Sweet!" he said. "A little too sweet, but still."

"You're Marcus Mandrake, the Harrington DJ!" I said with a smile.

"Marcus owes me a favor," Ross said. "So I asked him to spin at your party tonight."

My mouth dropped open. "A real-live DJ?" I squeaked. "At Mary-Kate's party?"

Ross nodded. I threw my arms around his neck and gave him the biggest hug!

"Who's this party for, anyway?" Marcus asked, looking around. "Strawberry Shortcake?"

"It's for my sister, Mary-Kate," I explained. "She thinks it's for Lavender Duncan, because Mary-Kate can never be surprised. But she will be now!"

Marcus showed me a list of songs. They were perfect for Mary-Kate!

"We're all set," Marcus said. He made a twisting motion with both hands. "Just tell me when to unleash the technics!"

"Huh?" I asked.

"What time should I show up to spin?" Marcus asked.

"We're surprising Mary-Kate at seven o'clock," I explained. "So be here at six forty-five, sharp!"

"Check!" Marcus said.

The guys left the U just as Lavender walked in.

"Lavender, guess what?" I called out. "Marcus Mandrake is going to—"

"Omigosh!" Lavender gasped.

"What's wrong?" I asked.

"*Nothing* is wrong!" Lavender said as she looked around the room. "Mary-Kate did such an awesome job decorating this room!"

Lavender spotted the harp-and-violin CDs on the table. She picked one up and squealed, "*Tranquil Breezes*! My favorite!"

I rolled my eyes to the ceiling.

"Lavender, I told you a million times," I said. "This party isn't for you—it's for Mary-Kate."

"I know that," Lavender said with a smile.

"So all this stuff isn't right for Mary-Kate," I added. "It's totally wrong for her."

"I know that, too," Lavender said, but she didn't sound disappointed.

I stared at Lavender as she left the U. Was the heat from her glue gun affecting her brain, or what?

But I wasn't as worried anymore.

Okay, I thought. *So Mary-Kate will hate the lacy tablecloths, the heart-shaped balloons, and the garlands. But she's going to love the cake and the tunes. And maybe her party won't be a total goof-up after all!*

Dear Diary,

I could hardly look at Mr. Patino in my history class today. Especially since he was wearing a TEACHER OF THE YEAR T-shirt his family had given him.

If that wasn't bad enough, everyone in school kept reminding me that the special assembly is tomorrow. As if I'm not thinking about it practically every second of the day!

I tried to escape everyone by retreating to my room during midday break. That's when Ms. Viola the housemother told me I had a phone call from Dad.

"Hi, sweetie!" Dad said over the phone. "I just want to wish you luck and tell you I'll be in New Hampshire tomorrow morning. In plenty of time for your special assembly."

"Cool!" I said.

"I told all my coworkers you aced the statewide history test, Mary-Kate," Dad said. "As your dad, I think I have bragging rights!"

Candles, Cake, Celebrate!

Diary, I wanted Dad to visit us more than ever. But I felt as if he was coming all the way here for nothing!

"Are you *sure* you want to come in for this assembly, Dad?" I asked.

"What do you mean?" Dad asked.

"Mrs. Pritchard's speeches last forever," I said. "And I'm sure Mr. Patino will go on and on and on talking, too."

"I've worked in a college, Mary-Kate," Dad chuckled. "I'm used to long speeches."

"Okay, but the seats in the auditorium," I went on frantically, "are *totally* lumpy!"

"I'm used to lumpy auditorium seats, too!" Dad said and laughed.

"And I heard the coffee at the inn tastes like swamp water!" I said. "There might even be a snowstorm in the next few . . . hours!"

"I'll just rent a team of huskies!" Dad joked. "You know I wouldn't miss this assembly for anything."

I felt someone tap my shoulder. I spun around and saw chatty Nora Banks.

"You've been on the phone forever!" Nora complained. "I have to call my mom. I lost my retainer and if I don't get a replacement I'm going to—"

"Hang on," I said. "It's my turn now."

I turned back to the phone and to my dad.

"Mary-Kate?" Dad's voice said. "Are you there?"

"I'm here." I sighed.

Diary, I was always able to talk to Dad about anything. And I wanted so badly to tell him the truth. "Dad, you're a biology professor," I said, speaking low so Nora couldn't hear me. "Did you ever make a mistake in grading a paper? Or a test?"

"Sure," Dad said. "About a year ago I marked a test grade correct when it was really incorrect."

Wow! I thought. *Dad made a mistake, too. Just like Mr. Patino!*

"Were you embarrassed?" I asked.

"A bit," Dad said. "But everyone makes mistakes. And I was glad the student brought it to my attention. Now I'm extra careful when I grade tests."

"Wait a minute," I said. "Did you just say your *student* told you about the mistake?"

"Yes," Dad said. "And I appreciated her honesty."

Hey, I thought. *If I tell Mr. Patino about his mistake, maybe he'll appreciate my honesty, too.*

A tap on my shoulder—again!

"What?" I asked. I whirled around and gulped. A whole *line* of girls was waiting to use the phone now! "Got to go, Dad," I said into the phone. "See you tomorrow."

Candles, Cake, Celebrate!

I hung up the phone and walked back to my room.

Change of plans! I thought. *I'm going to tell Mr. Patino the truth about the test* before *he goes home today. But first, I'm going to tell Ashley!*

Chapter 10

Later Monday

Dear Diary,

You're not going to believe what happened. Not in a gazillion years.

It was six o'clock. Phoebe and I were getting dressed for Mary-Kate's surprise party. We were going with the big movie-star look, even if there would be parasols around the room. I was tying a polka-dotted sash around the waist of my black dress. Phoebe looked like a 1920s movie star in her vintage flapper dress and long beaded necklace.

"Just think, Phoebe," I said. "In an hour I'll be surprising Mary-Kate. For the first time in our lives!"

Suddenly there was a knock on the door!

"It's probably Wendy," I said. "She always wants to borrow my iron."

But when I opened the door, I saw Mary-Kate. She was standing in the hall dressed in jeans, sneakers, and a long-sleeved tee!

"Hi, Ashley," Mary-Kate said.

I tried to keep my voice calm as I asked, "Why aren't you dressed for Lavender's party? You *are* going, aren't you?"

"Sure," Mary-Kate said, walking past me into the room. "But I have to tell you something first."

"Is it private?" Phoebe asked. "Should I leave?"

"No," Mary-Kate said. "Everybody is going to find out sooner or later, anyway."

Find out what? I wondered.

The springs of my mattress squeaked a little as Mary-Kate sat on my bed. She picked up my stuffed zebra and took a deep breath.

"Mr. Patino made a mistake when he graded my test," Mary-Kate said. "He marked my last answer right when it was really wrong. So I didn't get one hundred percent, I got ninety-eight percent."

Phoebe and I both stared at Mary-Kate.

"You didn't get all the answers right?" I asked slowly.

"No," Mary-Kate said. "And that means I'm not the history champ."

My mouth dropped open. I couldn't believe it.

"How do you know?" Phoebe asked.

Mary-Kate pulled out a paper and unfolded it. "Here's the copy of my test," I said. "The right answer to the last question is 'd.' And I wrote 'a.'"

Phoebe and I studied the test. Mary-Kate was right. She had written the wrong answer.

"I'm sorry, Mary-Kate," I said, sitting beside her. "This must be a huge letdown."

"It is," Mary-Kate admitted. "But I can't go on pretending I'm the history champ when I'm really not."

Not the history champ?

Suddenly it hit me. . . .

"If you're not the history champ," I said, "then what about the special assembly tomorrow? And Dad?"

"And the par—" Phoebe started to say until I jabbed her with my elbow!

"I know. I wasn't sure whether to wait until afterward or not. But now I'm sure," Mary-Kate said. She tossed my zebra to the side and stood up. "First I'm going to find Mr. Patino so I can tell him the truth."

Phoebe and I were silent as Mary-Kate left the room. The second the door slammed shut, we turned to each other.

"The party is in an hour, Phoebe!" I cried. "The DJ is all set to come!"

"The cake is on the way, too!" Phoebe wailed. "So are our friends!"

"Oh, no!" I groaned. "If Mary-Kate doesn't get this special assembly, what's the point in throwing her a surprise party?"

Dear Diary,

The copy of my test fluttered in my shaking hands as I walked to Mr. Patino's office. I knew I was doing the right thing. But I was still a nervous wreck!

Candles, Cake, Celebrate!

I stopped in front of his classroom. I stood on my toes and peeked through the small window on the door. The light was on, and Mr. Patino was inside. He was standing behind his desk packing his briefcase.

Here goes, I thought. I reached out to knock on the door. But then—

"Mary-Kate! Mary-Kate!"

I whirled around. Ashley was racing down the hall toward me.

"What is it?" I asked.

Ashley stopped at my side and declared, "I'm here to support you."

"Thanks," I said. But when I turned back toward the door, Ashley grabbed my arm.

"Are you sure you want to do this?" Ashley blurted out. "I mean, think of the school. Everyone is so psyched about the special assembly tomorrow! And Dad is leaving a major project to come in all the way from South Carolina! And Mr. Patino is getting an award, too! Think about all that, Mary-Kate!"

"I have been thinking about all of that. For *days*!" I smiled. "And you call this support?"

I knocked on the door.

"Come in!" Mr. Patino's voice called.

Mr. Patino smiled at me as I opened the door. I stepped into his classroom, with Ashley right behind me.

"Hi, Mary-Kate!" Mr. Patino said. "Hi, Ashley."

I stepped closer to Mr. Patino's desk and said, "Before you say anything, Mr. Patino, let me tell you something really important."

"Okay," Mr. Patino said, sitting down.

"I didn't get one hundred percent on the history test," I began.

Mr. Patino looked surprised. He listened quietly as I told him everything. When I finished, his eyebrows knotted and he said, "I could have sworn you got the last answer right, Mary-Kate. It was a trick question, and you wrote 'd' for 'New York City'."

"You see? You got it right!" Ashley said, pulling my arm. "Now let's go!"

I pulled my arm back. Then I handed Mr. Patino the copy of my test. "See for yourself, Mr. Patino," I said.

Mr. Patino studied the paper. Then he placed it on his desk and walked to his file cabinet.

What's he doing? I wondered.

"Here's your original test, Mary-Kate," Mr. Patino said. He pulled it out, looked at it, and grinned. Then he handed it to me and said, "There! Proof positive."

Ashley peered over my shoulder as we both looked at the test. Written next to the last question was a—

Candles, Cake, Celebrate!

"'D'?" I asked. "I did write a 'd'?"

"Then . . . how?" Ashley started to say.

"I think I have a hunch," Mr. Patino said. "I kept your original test to show to the state judges and I made a photocopy for you. Now take a look at this." He showed us a memo that he had gotten from Mrs. Pritchard's office last Tuesday.

"The memo is a photocopy, too," Mr. Patino said. "As you can see, the 'b' in this sentence looks like an 'o.' And it's on the bottom of the page, around the same spot as the last question on your test."

Mr. Patino placed the two papers back-to-back. Then he held it up to the light and said, "See?"

"A perfect match!" Ashley exclaimed.

"But how did it happen, Mr. Patino?" I asked. "Why were the letters cut off like that?"

"I think I know," Ashley said suddenly. "There might have been a speck of dust on the glass of the copier. That sometimes happens to the *Acorn*'s copier, too."

"Well, Ashley!" Mr. Patino said. "I can see you're as smart as your sister!"

"Does this mean Mary-Kate is still the history champ?" Ashley asked.

"The one and only," Mr. Patino replied.

I breathed a sigh of relief. "Thanks, Mr. Patino!" I said. "I'll see you at the assembly tomorrow!"

Ashley and I slipped out the door. When we were in the hall, we held hands and jumped up and down.

"I'm still a genius!" I exclaimed.

"Get over yourself," Ashley giggled, but she was still jumping up and down.

"All that worrying for nothing!" I said. "Now I can have my special assembly!"

"Yeah!" Ashley said. "And your surprise par—" She clapped her hand over her mouth and mumbled, "Whoops."

"Ashley?" I asked slowly. "Did you just say *my* surprise party?"

Ashley uncovered her mouth, cracked a nervous smile, and squeaked, "Did I?"

Something was definitely up!

"Ashley, what's going on?" I asked. "I thought this surprise party was for Lavender."

"It is!" Ashley said. "I mean, it was. I mean . . . " Her shoulders dropped, and she sighed. Then she said, "Okay, Mary-Kate. The surprise party tonight is for you. But we pretended it was for Lavender so you wouldn't have a clue."

"Why'd you do that?" I asked.

"Because I wanted to surprise you!" Ashley exclaimed. "For the first time in our lives! And now I can't believe that I'm the one who blew it!"

Candles, Cake, Celebrate!

I smiled at my sister. I couldn't believe she had gone through all that trouble just to surprise me. "You did surprise me, Ashley!" I said.

"I did?" Ashley asked.

"Sure!" I said. "All this time you had me thinking the party *was* for Lavender. And all this time it was really for me!"

Ashley waited a beat. Then she pumped her fist in the air and shouted, "Yippee! I did it! I did it!"

"Shh!" I giggled. "We're in the hall, not the U!"

"The U!" Ashley gasped. She looked at her watch. "I just remembered. Everyone's probably waiting there. To surprise you!"

"I can still act surprised," I said. "Let's go!"

Ashley looked at my grungy T-shirt and jeans and frowned. "Dressed like that?" she asked.

"Ashley!" I said with a laugh. "It's supposed to be a *surprise* party!"

We zipped up our parkas and ran across campus to the Student U building. Ashley opened the door and flicked on the lights.

"What a sur—" I stopped in mid-sentence and looked around the U.

No one was jumping out and yelling "surprise," because no one was there!

"Where is everybody?" Ashley asked. "Where are our friends? And the DJ? And the guys?"

"I don't know," I said. But as I looked around the U at the wicker baskets, dried flowers, lacy table-cloths, and heart-shaped balloons, I groaned. "Ashley, I can't have a party like this!" I said.

"What?" Ashley asked.

"I know this party is for me," I said. "But it's so *not* me!"

Chapter 11

Later Monday

Dear Diary,

What good is finally surprising your sister when she ditches her own surprise party?

"I was afraid of this, Mary-Kate!" I groaned. "You kept picking out stuff that was right for Lavender but wrong for yourself."

"Then why didn't you stop me?" Mary-Kate asked.

"I tried!" I insisted.

"Hi, there!" a voice said.

Mary-Kate and I spun around. Lavender was standing in the doorway. She was wearing a gingham dress, and her hair was hanging in two long braids.

"Omigosh, Lavender!" I cried. "You look like Dorothy from *The Wizard of Oz!*"

Lavender clicked the heels of her red shoes together and said, "There's no place like a party! There's no place like a party—"

"Yeah, and speaking of the party, I was right all along," I cut in. "Mary-Kate doesn't want a party like this."

Lavender turned to Mary-Kate. "I don't blame

you, Mary-Kate," she said. "Baskets, dried flowers, and parasols are more my style than yours."

"Now you tell her!" I said.

"Oh, well," Mary-Kate said. "This won't be much of a party, anyway. Nobody's here."

Lavender waved her hand toward the door. "Mary-Kate, Ashley," she said. "Follow me."

"Where is she taking us?" I whispered as we followed Lavender down the hall. "The Emerald City?"

When Lavender reached the teachers' lounge, she stopped. She pushed open the door, waved us inside, and—

"SURPRISE!!"

I froze as I stared around the room. Silver and black balloons were hanging everywhere. Gold cardboard stars with students' names on them were dangling from the ceiling. A long table on one side of the room was filled with bowls of chips, onion rings, fried chicken, and guacamole dip. All of Mary-Kate's favorite foods!

I smiled at our friends. They were dressed like movie characters, too. Elise looked just like Catwoman, in a stretch leotard, hood, and whiskers. Wendy was wearing a trenchcoat and forties-style hat straight out of a Hollywood mystery film. Jordan and Ross looked like the Men in Black with their dark sunglasses and suits. Phoebe's flapper outfit already made her look like a silent film star! Everyone looked amazing!

It's the Hollywood party theme! I thought. *The one I wanted for Mary-Kate!*

"Quiet on the set!" Campbell shouted. She stepped forward, wearing a baseball uniform. But she held up a director's clapboard and said, "History Champ's surprise party. Take two!"

A blast of rock music filled the room. Marcus was off to the side.

"Surprised?" Lavender asked with a grin.

"For the second time in my whole life!" Mary-Kate said.

"You surprised me, too," I admitted. "But how . . . when . . . ?"

"Everyone knows how much I love planning parties," Lavender said. "So I secretly planned Mary-Kate's party on my own. I picked out all the supplies, even the costumes from the theater department. And I didn't tell anyone until they showed up in the Student U."

"But why didn't you tell me?" I asked.

"It was more fun this way!" Lavender said. "So was pretending that Mary-Kate was picking out the right things for her party when they were all so wrong."

"That's why you kept egging me on!" Mary-Kate said. "But how did you get to use the teachers' lounge?"

"Yeah," I said. "Students are never allowed to hang out in here."

"Mrs. Pritchard gave me permission to use it," Lavender said. "After I promised to bake my famous lemon squares for the Alumni Tea next month."

I suddenly remembered the party supplies in the Student U. "What's going to happen to all that other stuff we bought?" I asked. "The flower baskets, doilies, parasols——"

"Well . . . " Lavender said, twirling her braid and smiling, "we can still celebrate the launch of my Web site."

"Good idea," I said. "We'll have it on Saturday afternoon. And we'll invite everyone who's here today."

I watched as she turned to the others. "Isn't this awesome, everyone?" Lavender called out. "Not only did we surprise Mary-Kate, we surprised Ashley, too!"

That's for sure! I thought.

Mary-Kate and I joined Jordan and Ross at the snack table. They were piling their plates high with potato salad and honey-barbecued chicken.

Candles, Cake, Celebrate!

"Lyle says he's sorry he couldn't make it to the party," Jordan said. "He and the football team are cramming for the Harrington history test tomorrow."

"Which is what we should be doing," Ross said. He grabbed a fistful of nacho chips. "But who can study on an empty stomach?"

The guys squirted ketchup on their onion rings. Everyone else was busy dancing to the beat of Marcus's amazing mixes.

"So how does it feel to be surprised finally?" I asked my sister as we carried our plates over to the sofa.

"I definitely like surprises!" Mary-Kate said. "There's just one problem with this party."

"Really?" I asked. "What?"

Mary-Kate nodded at all of our dancing friends. "We're the only ones not wearing Hollywood-movie costumes!" she said.

"You're right," I said.

Suddenly I spotted two giant rubber cowboy hats hanging on a wall. The cowboy hats we had seen at the Party Hearty store! The ones Mary-Kate wouldn't let me buy.

I ran to grab them. Then I dropped them over our heads. "Westerns are huge in Hollywood, you know," I said. "Now let's party!"

"Yee-haa!" Mary-Kate cheered.

Diary, it was the perfect party!

And everything worked out after all. Mary-Kate did ace the statewide history test. And I finally got to surprise my sister.

Chapter 12

Tuesday, Assembly Day

Dear Diary,

Today's the big day—the day of the special award assembly!

I must be the happiest student in New Hampshire. Well, *one* of the happiest. During midday break Lyle told me he had passed the Harrington history test!

"So did the other guys you tutored!" Lyle said.

"How do you know?" I asked.

"The headmaster told us right after they graded the tests this morning," Lyle said. "He said we can all stay on the football team, too!"

I threw both fists in the air and shouted, "Touchdown!"

As if that wasn't cool enough, Ashley and my friends surprised me during lunch with a bouquet of yellow roses. Yeah, Diary, I did say *surprised*!

But after giving me the roses, Ashley gave me some bad news.

"Dad's plane is delayed," Ashley said. "He left a message for us that he might be late."

"You mean he might miss the assembly?" I asked.

"Maybe," Ashley said.

My heart sank. What if Dad missed the special

assembly? Getting my certificate wouldn't be the same without him there.

"Thanks for the roses, you guys," I said.

Lavender leaned across the lunch table and said, "Did you know that roses can be everlasting? You can dry them. Or press the rosebuds between the pages of a book!"

"Great tip," I said with a smile. "But for now, I'll just stick them in a vase."

I tried my best not to worry about Dad during lunch or my next two classes. When it was finally two thirty, Ashley and I walked over to the auditorium together.

"Do you think Dad is here already?" I asked.

Ashley showed me her crossed fingers.

But when we walked into the auditorium— no Dad!

Ashley sat in the first row. She saved the seat next to her by plopping her backpack onto it. I sat on the stage between Mrs. Pritchard and Mrs. Patino. A movie screen had been set up a few feet away from our chairs. That's where they would show my test.

I looked into the audience. The whole First Form was there, including my friends. Ross and Jordan were there, too. So was Lyle—and the whole Harrington football team!

Candles, Cake, Celebrate!

"Mary-Kate! Mary-Kate! Mary-Kate!" the guys cheered.

Mrs. Pritchard walked up to the microphone. "Boys!" she scolded. "This is an award ceremony, not a pep rally!"

The guys piped down. I couldn't stop staring at the empty seat in the first row and wondering, "Where's Dad?"

"We'll start the assembly with a short film about American history," Mrs. Pritchard said. "It's called *From Sea to Shining Sea*."

The lights went out in the auditorium. I sat back in my chair and watched the movie.

Not bad, I thought. *For an assembly movie*.

When the movie ended the lights flashed on. I blinked my eyes to adjust to the bright light. But when I turned in my chair to face the audience I gasped. Sitting in the once-empty seat next to Ashley was—

"Dad!" I whispered.

Dad gave me a little wave. And Ashley gave me a big thumbs-up sign!

He made it! I thought. *He made it!*

Mrs. Pritchard stepped up to the mike again. It was time to honor Mr. Patino. The Patino family cheered and whistled as he was handed a certificate and a baseball cap that read #1 TEACHER.

Mr. Patino made a speech about how much he loves teaching. He even thanked his mom for making him study so hard as a kid!

"Speaking of studying," Mr. Patino said. "It's time to honor the student who proved that hard work really does pay off."

Mrs. Pritchard held up a framed certificate.

"Let's give it up for the statewide history champ," Mr. Patino said. "White Oak's very own . . . Mary-Kate Burke!"

"Yay!" Ashley cheered.

I stood up as cheers and whistles filled the auditorium. Lyle and the football team held up a banner that read GO MARY-KATE!

"Atta girl, Mary-Kate!" Dad shouted.

Mrs. Pritchard handed me the certificate. "Congratulations, Mary-Kate," she said. "Keep up the good work."

"Thanks, Mrs. Pritchard," I said.

I smiled down at the certificate. Now I had something else to hang over my desk. And this time it wasn't a photocopy.

It was the *real deal*!

And now that my special assembly is over, it's time to celebrate with Dad and my sister at that cool hamburger restaurant Ashley picked out just for me!

Candles, Cake, Celebrate!

"This place will have everything you love, Mary-Kate," Ashley said as we walked out of Porter House. "It'll have barbecued chicken, pictures of famous rockers on the walls, way-cool music—"

"And, best of all," I said with a smile, "Dad!"

Dear Diary:

Today, I got the coolest assignment from Ms. Hong, my social sciences teacher.

We're doing a unit on animal behavior—and we get to study and take care of a real live animal!

Each of us has been assigned to a different animal-care place. We have to observe the animal's diet, habits, relationships with other animals nearby—whatever we see. And this is the best part of all: I'm working at Starbright Stables. I get to take care of my very own . . . you guessed it . . . HORSE!

But I'm not taking care of a horse by myself, Diary. Everyone in class is working with a partner. I was really hoping to work with one of my friends, but instead I've been paired up with Courtney

Spaulding. I don't know her very well—she's new here. She seems pretty nice so far. At least, that's what I thought.

At the end of class today, I looked around for Courtney. I wanted to talk about the assignment, and get to know her better.

After all the other kids cleared out, I finally spotted her over by Ms. Hong's desk, deep in conversation with our teacher. I slowly wandered over to the front of the room. As I did, I couldn't help overhearing what Courtney was saying.

"Do I have to?" Courtney asked. "If you could give me anything else to do. Please, Ms. Hong, couldn't you change it? I'll work with anyone else—"

I inched closer so I could hear better. But Ms. Hong looked up at that moment and caught my eye. My face flamed, and I quickly gazed away.

"Courtney, let's talk more about this in my office," she said.

As Ms. Hong picked up her books, Courtney turned around and saw me standing there.

"Mary-Kate!" Courtney gasped. She blushed and gave me a worried look. Then she turned quickly and followed Ms. Hong out of the room.

I stood there, wondering what was going on. Courtney was clearly very upset.

She definitely didn't want this assignment. But was it because of Starbright Stables?

Or was it because of me?

Dear Diary,

Guess what? Today was the day Mrs. Pritchard chose the two new girls to work in her office!

Every term, Mrs. Pritchard hires two of the White Oak first-formers to work in her office. It's a great job and tons of kids want it. Including me. I submitted my application months ago.

This morning in assembly, Mrs. Pritchard was going to announce which two girls had been chosen. As I raced into the auditorium with Phoebe, Mary-Kate, and Campbell, I overheard Dana Woletsky talking to Kristen Lindquist and Fiona Ferris.

"She's almost sure to pick me," Dana was saying. "After all, my mother was a White Oak girl, and so was my grandmother. I don't know why I haven't gotten the job before now—"

I frowned. Dana was always bragging—especially about her family having gone to White Oak for forever. We walked past them and found seats. Dana and her friends sat down right behind us. It figures.

Then Mrs. Pritchard stood up on stage and walked to the podium. "Settle down, girls," she said, raising her hand. "Now, I know you're all curious to know who will be working in the office this month, so I'm not going to leave you in suspense."

I leaned forward in my seat. I really wanted the job!

"The two girls chosen are Ashley Burke . . ."

My sister whooped and gave me a quick hug. Campbell gave me a thumbs-up. A bunch of other girls turned around and smiled at me, too. I felt great!

Dana leaned forward. "Nice to have you working with me, Ashley," she said in a very loud whisper. You could hear her twenty rows away. Even Mrs. Pritchard looked over at her and raised her eyebrows.

Mrs. Pritchard waited until things settled down again. "My second helper this term is . . ." She looked down at a piece of paper in her hand. "Becky David."

The room fell silent. Heads swiveled, looking for Becky.

I turned around, too. Dana's face was bright red. Kristen was saying something to her, and Dana was shaking her head furiously.

I have to admit, Diary, I was surprised Mrs. Pritchard had chosen Becky. I didn't know her that well, but everyone says she's a bit of a klutz, and a little forgetful, too.

Mrs. Pritchard's voice interrupted my thoughts. "Anyway, that's it for this morning, girls," she finished. "Becky and Ashley, report to my office at three-thirty. Everybody, have a great day!"

As we filed out of the auditorium, I passed Becky. She was sitting in the back row, looking a little stunned, so I walked over to her.

"Hey, congratulations!" I said. "It'll be fun working with you!

"Thanks," Becky said in a sort of dazed voice.

"Yes. Congratulations, Becky." Becky and I both turned to see Dana standing there.

"I hope you do really well at the job," Dana said sweetly, looking at Becky. "Of course, if you run into any trouble . . . well, I'd be glad to help. My mom and grandmother both went here, so I know the ropes." Dana's eyes narrowed. "And I'd be happy to take over from you if anything goes wrong."

Becky froze. Dana just stared at her.

Sure, what Dana said sounded nice enough. But the way she said it . . . well, it sounded like some kind of threat. I knew Dana had counted on getting the job, but there wasn't anything she could do about it now.

Or was there?

Two of a Kind
"Win a Sterling Silver Charm Bracelet" Sweepstakes
OFFICIAL RULES:

1. **NO PURCHASE OR PAYMENT NECESSARY TO ENTER OR WIN.**

2. **How to Enter.** To enter, complete the official entry form or hand print your name, address, age, and phone number along with the words "*Two of a Kind* Win A Sterling Silver Charm Bracelet Sweepstakes" on a 3" x 5" card and mail to: "*Two of a Kind* Win A Sterling Silver Charm Bracelet Sweepstakes" c/o HarperEntertainment, Attn: Children's Marketing Department, 10 East 53rd Street, New York, NY 10022. Entries must be received no later than July 28, 2005. Enter as often as you wish, but each entry must be mailed separately. One entry per envelope. Partially completed, illegible, or mechanically reproduced entries will not be accepted. Sponsor is not responsible for lost, late, mutilated, illegible, stolen, postage due, incomplete, or misdirected entries. All entries become the property of Dualstar Entertainment Group, LLC, and will not be returned.

3. **Eligibility.** Sweepstakes are open to all legal residents of the United States (excluding Colorado and Rhode Island), who are between the ages of five and fifteen on July 28, 2005 excluding employees and immediate family members of HarperCollins Publishers, Inc., ("HarperCollins"), Parachute Properties and Parachute Press, Inc., and their respective subsidiaries and affiliates, officers, directors, shareholders, employees, agents, attorneys, and other representatives and their immediate families (individually and collectively, "Parachute"), Dualstar Entertainment Group, LLC, and its subsidiaries, affiliates and related companies, officers, directors, shareholders, employees, agents, attorneys, and other representatives and their immediate families (individually and collectively, "Dualstar"), and their respective parent companies, affiliates, subsidiaries, advertising, promotion and fulfillment agencies, and the persons with whom each of the above are domiciled. All applicable federal, state and local laws and regulations apply. Offer void where prohibited or restricted by law.

4. **Odds of Winning.** Odds of winning depend on the total number of entries received. Approximately 250,000 sweepstakes announcements published. All prizes will be awarded. Winners will be randomly drawn on or about August 15, 2005, by HarperCollins, whose decision is final. Potential winners will be notified by mail and will be required to sign and return an affidavit of eligibility and release of liability within 14 days of notification. Prize won by minors will be awarded to parent or legal guardian who must sign and return all required legal documents. By acceptance of the prize, winners consent to the use of their name, photograph, likeness, and biographical information by HarperCollins, Parachute, Dualstar, and for publicity purposes without further compensation except where prohibited.

5. **Grand-Prize. Twenty Grand-Prize Winners** will win a sterling silver charm bracelet. Approximate retail value is $100 per prize.

6. **Prize Limitations.** Prizes are non-transferable and cannot be sold or redeemed for cash. No cash substitute is available. Any federal, state, or local taxes are the responsibility of the winners. Sponsor may substitute prize of equal or greater value, if necessary, due to availability.

7. **Additional terms:** By participating, entrants agree a) to the official rules and decisions of the judges, which will be final in all respects; and to waive any claim to ambiguity of the official rules and b) to release, discharge, and hold harmless HarperCollins, Parachute, Dualstar, and their respective parent companies, affiliates, subsidiaries, employees and representatives and advertising, promotion and fulfillment agencies from and against any and all liability or damages associated with acceptance, use, or misuse of any prize received or participation in any Sweepstakes-related activity or participation in this Sweepstakes.

8. **Dispute Resolution.** Any dispute arising from this Sweepstakes will be determined according to the laws of the State of New York, without reference to its conflict of law principles, and the entrants consent to the personal jurisdiction of the State and Federal courts located in New York County and agree that such courts have exclusive jurisdiction over all such disputes.

9. **Winner Information.** To obtain the name of the winners, please send your request and a self-addressed stamped envelope (residents of Vermont may omit return postage) to "*Two of a Kind* Win A Sterling Silver Charm Bracelet Sweepstakes" Winner, c/o HarperEntertainment, 10 East 53rd Street, New York, NY 10022 after September 15, 2005, but no later than March 15, 2006.

10. **Sweepstakes Sponsor:** HarperCollins Publishers.